MAY - - 2022

WHERE
SNOW
ANGELS
GO

For Iris Zelda,
with love
MO

To my family, original and acquired, for all their practical
and emotional support. To my son, Mio, for making me
feel in love every day. And especially to Edith, for posing
so patiently for my Sylvie and letting me drag her
whole family into it, too.
DJT

Text copyright © 2020 by Maggie O'Farrell
Illustrations copyright © 2020 by Daniela Jaglenka Terrazzini

First US edition 2021

Library of Congress Catalog Card Number pending
ISBN 978-1-5362-1937-1

21 22 23 24 25 26 APS 10 9 8 7 6 5 4 3 2 1

Printed in Humen, Dongguan, China

This book was typeset in Berkeley Oldstyle.
The illustrations were done in ink and watercolor.

Candlewick Press
99 Dover Street
Somerville, Massachusetts 02144

www.candlewick.com

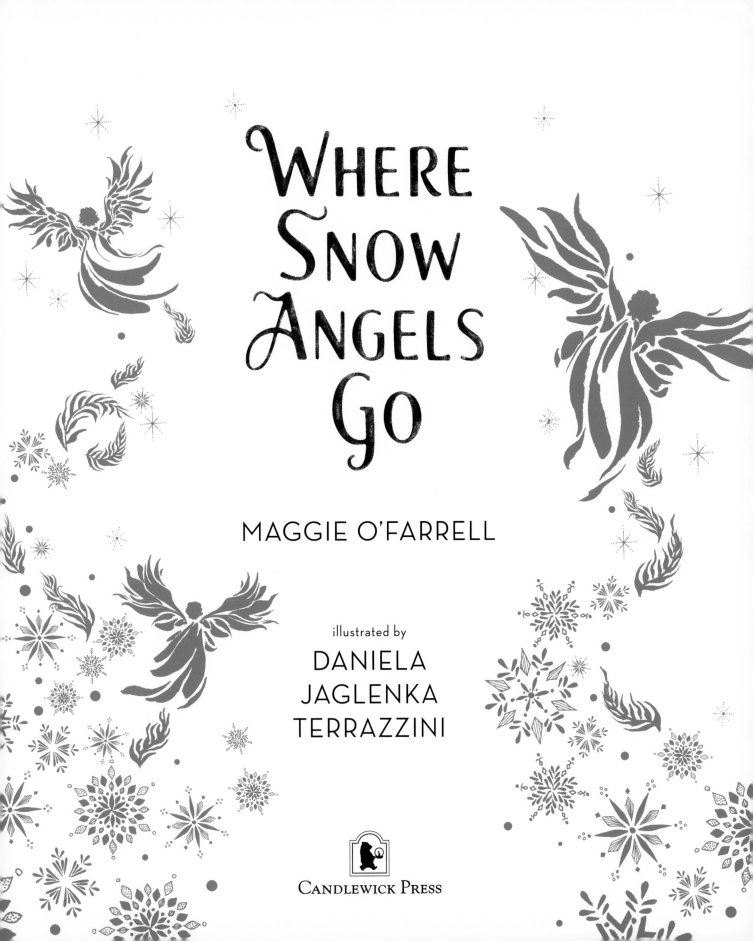

WHERE SNOW ANGELS GO

MAGGIE O'FARRELL

illustrated by

DANIELA JAGLENKA TERRAZZINI

CANDLEWICK PRESS

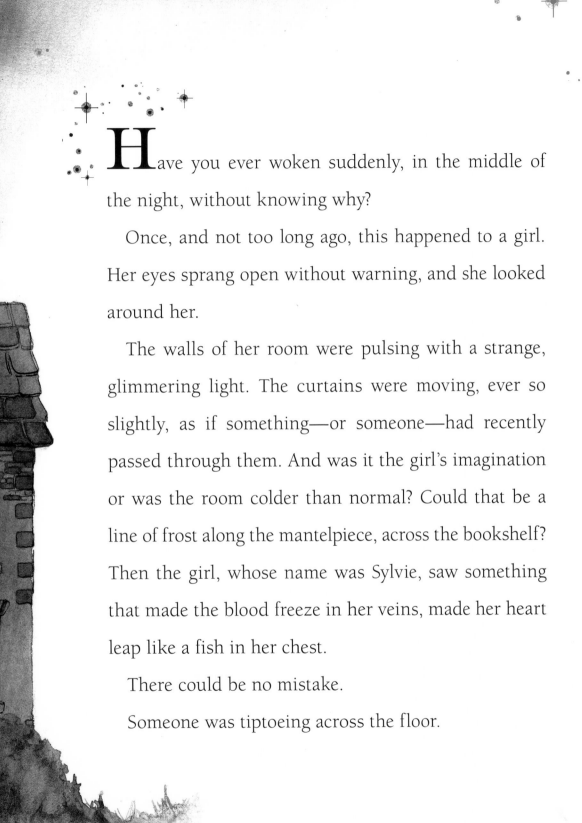

Have you ever woken suddenly, in the middle of the night, without knowing why?

Once, and not too long ago, this happened to a girl. Her eyes sprang open without warning, and she looked around her.

The walls of her room were pulsing with a strange, glimmering light. The curtains were moving, ever so slightly, as if something—or someone—had recently passed through them. And was it the girl's imagination or was the room colder than normal? Could that be a line of frost along the mantelpiece, across the bookshelf? Then the girl, whose name was Sylvie, saw something that made the blood freeze in her veins, made her heart leap like a fish in her chest.

There could be no mistake.

Someone was tiptoeing across the floor.

His outline shimmered with a moonlike glow, his skin a strange blue-white. Most incredible by far was what extended from his back: a pair of wings, enormous in size, and made of the softest snow-white feathers imaginable.

He was picking his way through her room, muttering to himself, wings wafting behind him.

"First, save the person," Sylvie could hear him say, "then fly down . . . No, that's not right . . . Find the . . . No, hang on . . . First, fly down. Second, find the person.

Third . . ." He shook his head, muddled, shutting his eyes, as if for inspiration. "Now, what comes third? I've forgotten and I really—"

Sylvie drew in a breath. She let it out. She drew in another and said, in a hoarse voice, "Excuse me."

The visitor whipped around, letting out a shriek, as if he'd accidentally trodden on something sharp.

"Heavens," he said, clutching at his chest, "you scared me. I was just . . ." He stopped and took a sideways step closer to the end of her bed. There was a short pause.

He stared at her with big, frightened eyes.

"You can see me?" he whispered, incredulous.

Sylvie nodded, looking up at him, holding the covers very tightly.

The visitor seemed utterly confused. He opened his mouth, as if he might speak, then he shut it again. He waved a hand up and down in front of his face, watching it so closely he looked cross-eyed for a moment. "Are you sure? I mean, *I* can see me. Can you?"

Sylvie laughed. She couldn't help herself. "Of course I can. I'm talking to you, aren't I?"

He let his hands fall to his sides. "Oh dear," he said in the saddest voice Sylvie had ever heard, his head hanging down dejectedly. "Oh no. I must have made

a mistake. I'm going to be in so much trouble. This is my first flight, you see, and I did want it to go well. I've no idea what I did wrong."

"I'm sure you didn't do anything wrong," Sylvie said kindly. He did seem very upset.

"But you're not supposed to be able to see me," he cried in despair. "And here you are"—he gestured at her—"seeing me. I tried so hard. I thought I'd done everything right, but"—he paused to let out an enormous misty sigh—"this isn't how it's meant to go."

"How is it meant to go?" Sylvie said.

"Well," he said, lowering himself to the chair at Sylvie's desk, "I fly down to find you, and I'm invisible, entirely invisible, while I save you, and then—"

"Save me?" Sylvie said. "From what?"

And then she uttered the question she'd been wanting to ask all along: "Who are you?"

He looked at the desk for a moment. He looked at the window, he looked at the row of wooden animals along the sill, he looked all around the room, and then back at Sylvie.

"I'm probably not even supposed to tell you. And," he said, "it's a long story."

He got up off Sylvie's chair and stretched. It was an astonishing sight. Sylvie had been told never to stare at people, but she couldn't help herself: his limbs were silvery blue, and his skin, under his thin white robe, seemed lit from within. His hair was sculpted curls of ice. When he moved, tiny showers of luminous dust came off him, like snow falling from a branch. He took

two steps towards the bed, and his wings
flexed out on either side of him.

"I am," he said from the foot of her bed,
"your snow angel."

"My what?" Sylvie said.

"Snow angel," he repeated.

"Snow what?"

"Sno-ow," he said, giving the word two
syllables, "an-gel. Are you having trouble
hearing me because—?"

"I can hear you," Sylvie said. "I've just
never heard of a snow angel."

"Not true," the snow angel said, folding his arms.

Sylvie drew herself up, as much as is possible while lying in bed. "It is true," she said. "I've never heard of such a thing and what's more—"

"But you made me," the angel said, his feathers ruffling and twitching.

"I did not. I . . . I can't have . . ." Sylvie stammered, but at the same time her mind was working, whirring, taking her back.

All the way back to last winter, to a day so silent it was as if a blanket had fallen over the world. A blizzard had blown through overnight and covered everything in cold whiteness. Sylvie, in bed, recalled a moment when she was leaning back in the snow, sweeping her arms and legs through its cold powder. Back and forth, back and forth. There were flakes on her eyelashes and on her lips, and she was laughing.

Sylvie gazed at the angel at the end of her bed. She looked all the way from the icy tip of his wings to his opalescent feet. "That was you?" she asked.

The snow angel inclined his head. "That was me. And when the snow melted the following day—"

"You disappeared," Sylvie said. "You were gone."

"Evaporated," the angel corrected, holding up a single finger, "not gone. I went up, molecule by molecule, into the air, to gather in the clouds. Once you make an angel in the snow," he said, "it is yours forever. We never disappear. We watch over you, the whole time, and come back whenever you need us."

"You watch over me?"

"Yes."

"From a cloud? In the sky?"

The angel tilted his head. "More or less."

"But how?"

He shrugged. "Things made of water or snow or ice are indestructible. If the sun comes out and dries us up, we just re-form elsewhere in the atmosphere. You've probably learned as much at school. It's simple science."

Sylvie giggled. "Science? An angel I made last winter reappearing in my room is science?"

The angel looked affronted. "Certainly. Do you doubt it?"

Sylvie laced her hands together. "It's not that I doubt it. I didn't mean to be rude. It just seems a bit more . . . a bit more like magic."

"Magic?" the angel said, as if he hated the word. "Absolutely not. Do I look magic to you?"

Sylvie examined his celestial robes, his illuminated outline, his silver-blue face, his enormous wings. "Yes," she said. "You do."

The angel sighed and ran a distracted hand through his curls. "Look, we're getting sidetracked here," he said, more to himself than to her. "I really had no idea that you would be so talkative. All this science and magic stuff is beside the point when the point is . . . The point is . . ." He looked around himself wildly, as if trying to remember what he was doing here, in a house, in the middle of the night. Then it seemed to come back to him. He lifted his chin, he straightened his robes, he cleared his throat. "The point is, of course, that I am on a mission. My first one ever. I am here," he said in an announcing sort of way, "to help you."

Sylvie gave a puzzled smile. "But I'm fine. I don't need help. I'm at home, in bed. I'm perfectly safe. Let's carry on chatting. Tell me more. What's it like up there in the sky? Why are you taller than the angel I made? Did the simple science make you stretch? What do you do all the time? Are there others like you? Are you all friends?"

The angel didn't seem to hear these questions. He was chewing his lip, looking at Sylvie very intently. He walked one way around the bed, then the other. He leaned in close, he drew back, he leaned in again.

"You're not *entirely* safe," he said eventually.

"I'm not?"

He shook his head. "I wouldn't be here if you were. Snow angels," he said with a hint of pride, "never make mistakes. At least not about this sort of thing. I think perhaps you're not very well."

"Really?" said Sylvie. "I feel fine."

"Hmm. You might feel fine, but you're not." He passed his hands through the air above her. Glittering snow dust showered down from him, falling onto her, soft as swans' down. Sylvie lay in her bed and watched as her snow angel stood above her, wings aloft, his face alert and concerned, his hands moving to and fro.

Sylvie reached up and took one of them. His fingers were cool and strong as marble. She found she wanted to place them on her forehead, just to feel them there, and so she did. There was a distinct fizzling sound as cold palm met hot brow.

"Aha," he murmured. "I knew it. I knew you weren't well. You have a fever."

Sylvie blinked underneath the hand.

"I'm going to have to wake up your mother. She'll know what to do."

He moved on his silent white feet towards the door.

"Snow Angel," Sylvie whispered, "are you coming back?"

He smiled, for the first time. "I never go away," he said. "In the morning, you won't remember any of this. That's the way things are with snow angels. You never see us, you never remember us. Or if you do, you'll just think you had a strange dream. But I'll always be here, watching out for you."

Sylvie saw him leave, saw him pass through the doorway, saw the bluish lustrous glow fade.

In the other room, Sylvie's mum woke with a start. She lay there for a moment, wondering what might have woken her and why the room was so cold, then she thought: I'll just go and check on Sylvie.

Sylvie was ill for a long time. She lay in bed for the whole summer, the entire autumn, and most of the winter. She was still in bed, most unfortunately, on Christmas Day. By the time the spring bulbs were pushing their green spears out of the soil, however, she was beginning to feel stronger. It wasn't long before she could go outside again.

The snow angel had been wrong about one thing. Sylvie did not forget about his visit: it was burned into her memory as clearly as if it had just happened. She could remember every detail about him, every single word he had said. She didn't tell anyone about her snow angel—not her mother, not her father, not her friends at school—but she thought about him every day.

She whispered his name to herself sometimes, under her breath, especially when she was alone. She hoped he would visit her again soon. There were many things she wanted to ask him. She hoped he hadn't got into trouble for talking to her. She wondered if he had worked out how to make himself invisible. Surely he would come to see her, now that she was better? They had so much to talk about. She would tell him about what it had been like to be ill for so long, about the people she met in hospital, how the doctor had said it had been very good luck that her mother woke up that night. She imagined that they would laugh together about that. "Luck?" he might say. "It was simple science."

She filled the margins of her schoolbooks with pictures of clouds, snowflakes, huge pairs of white wings. She waited for him to visit again; she waited and watched, and waited some more.

But the snow angel didn't come.

One day, Sylvie was at school. She was supposed to be listening to the teacher, who was telling them a story about their town in the olden days, but she was, in fact, sketching a line of clouds across the top of her book.

If the snow angel watched her all the time, she thought to herself, then he was watching her now. He could see her at this very moment, sitting in class. He was watching her draw a figure with wings and a robe, standing on top of a cloud, gazing down to earth. And if, she thought, something dangerous were to happen to her—a hungry monster bursting in through the classroom door, for example, or a sudden flood lifting their tables and chairs from the ground—then he would have to come down.

Sylvie chewed the end of her pencil, struck by this idea. She was just about to erase the figure and draw him taking to the air, wings extended, when, out of the blue, the teacher asked her a question. Sylvie had to banish all thoughts of angels and clouds, put down her pencil, and pretend that she had been listening all along.

After school, Sylvie decided to push things, just a little, to see if she could make her snow angel appear. She wanted to see him, and she had a feeling he would want to see her. It was probably quite dull to be up there in the sky all the time, day after day, just looking down. Wasn't it the kindest thing, really, to give him something to do?

On the way home, she looked for the tallest tree in the park. She climbed it and climbed it and climbed it, and when she reached the top, she shunted herself to the end of a long branch. She couldn't look down, couldn't bear to see the faraway grass, the distant swings, the tiny people walking along the path. She shut her eyes, gripped the branch tight and made herself bounce up and down. Look at me, she wanted to call, I might fall, I really might.

Nothing happened. She just felt a bit sick, and after a while, she climbed down and went home.

The next day, she made
herself hang upside-down by
one leg from a tire swing and swayed
back and forth. She took to walking
around the house with her eyes shut and her
arms outstretched, bumping into things. She
tobogganed down the stairs on a tea tray.

She went right up to the biggest boy at school and told him he was a bully and that he should stop tripping people up. The boy was so astonished that Sylvie was able to run away before he tried to catch her.

Nothing worked. The snow angel never came. Sylvie thought that maybe he had forgotten about her. Or had she dreamed him after all?

Then, right at the end of summer, Sylvie was
swimming at the seaside, when a wave went over her
head. She found herself suddenly out of her depth,
under the water, and she didn't know which way was

up and she couldn't touch the bottom with her feet and the shore seemed very distant indeed. She couldn't open her mouth to call for help because she didn't want to swallow seawater, and she knew her parents were too far away to hear.

She was gripped by a terrible panic. Who would save her? All she could see were water and bubbles and confusing splinters of light. She seemed to be still moving out to sea, and she was thinking that she might never reach the air again, that her time was up, when she felt another wave take hold of her.

This wave was different.

It was strong, it was decisive. It snatched her from the clutches of the current and pulled her back the other way, towards the shore. Sylvie felt her hair swirling about her as she was carried along; she saw the surface of the sea coming down to meet her. Suddenly, her head broke up out of the water and she could take in gulps of air.

There she was, back on the beach, in the shallows, sitting upright, coughing and spluttering. She hadn't been swept out, she hadn't been lost at sea. The day was still sunny and people were still building sandcastles on the shore and the ice-cream van was still playing its tune. Her mother and father and the dog were running down the beach, worried looks on their faces, and they were getting themselves tangled up in the dog's lead because they were all determined to be the first to reach her.

Sylvie's mother wrapped her in a towel and gave her a hot drink. The dog helpfully climbed onto her knee for a nap. Sylvie sat on the beach and thought about that second wave. There was something special about it. Something different. It had been much colder than all the others. And was it her imagination or had she felt the soft, brushing sensation of feathers as it propelled her towards land?

HELP!

Not long after this, Sylvie was riding her bike down a steep hill when she realized she couldn't slow down. The brakes didn't seem to be working and her bike wheels were whirring and she was heading for the train tracks at the bottom of the hill.

The word "Help!" stretched out from her mouth, as if on elastic, and suddenly there was a big gust of wind.

It pushed Sylvie sideways, tipping her off her speeding bike and into a pile of leaves, headfirst. Sylvie watched as her bike continued on down the hill all on its own.

She was quiet as she pushed her mangled bike home.
She was thoughtful at teatime. She barely said a word
during her bath.

Later that night, she got out of bed, pulled back her curtains, and peered upwards. The sky was like a black cloth strewn with fragments of diamond. She pressed her warm fingertips to the cool glass and watched as condensation, minuscule droplets of water, spread out around them; she saw the steam of her breath appear and disappear as her chest rose and fell.

She knew now that the snow angel was there, with her, watching her, the whole time, just as he'd promised. She hadn't forgotten him, and she knew she never would.

She couldn't summon him by doing dangerous things; it didn't work like that. He only came when she really needed him, when she was looking the other way.

"Thank you," she whispered, sending her words up towards the sky.

There was no reply.

But Sylvie was sure—absolutely sure—that just for a moment, there was another reflection in the window alongside her own, a tall one, with great white wings, and he was shedding silver dust as he nodded at her.

When winter came around again, something occurred to Sylvie.

"Have you ever made a snow angel?" Sylvie asked her mother.

"A what?" her mother said.

Sylvie frowned and walked away. She went to everyone else she knew and asked them the same question.

"I'm on the phone, sweetheart," said her father. "Can we talk about this another time?"

"Pardon?" said her grandmother. "A slow angel, did you say?"

"I don't know, darling. Ask your mother," said her grandfather.

"Special deal on oranges today," said the man at the fruit stall.

"I've made a snow*man*," said her friend at school. "Does that count?"

Sylvie didn't think it did. She began to lie awake at night, wondering what might happen to all the people who didn't have a snow angel up there, looking after them, like she did. Who would save them if they were ever in danger?

"I don't want anything bad to happen to you," she told her mother as they walked to school.

Her mother took her hand. "Nothing bad is going to happen," she said.

"You don't know that," said Sylvie.

Her mother looked at her more closely.

"That's true. But you mustn't worry."

"You have to make yourself a snow angel," said Sylvie. "Will you do that? Do you promise?"

Her mother laughed and ruffled her hair. "You can't make a snow angel without snow."

That night, Sylvie stayed awake until she heard the town clock strike twelve. Then she tiptoed downstairs, through the kitchen, and out into the garden. There was a lacework of frost on the ground, and the moon was a polished coin in the sky. She stood in the middle of the lawn and tipped back her head.

"I need your help!"

she called out.

"Are you there?"

A rustle, a murmur, as a breeze passed through the trees.

"Where are you?" she called. "I know you can hear me." The garden was silent. Fast-moving clouds scrolled by over her head.

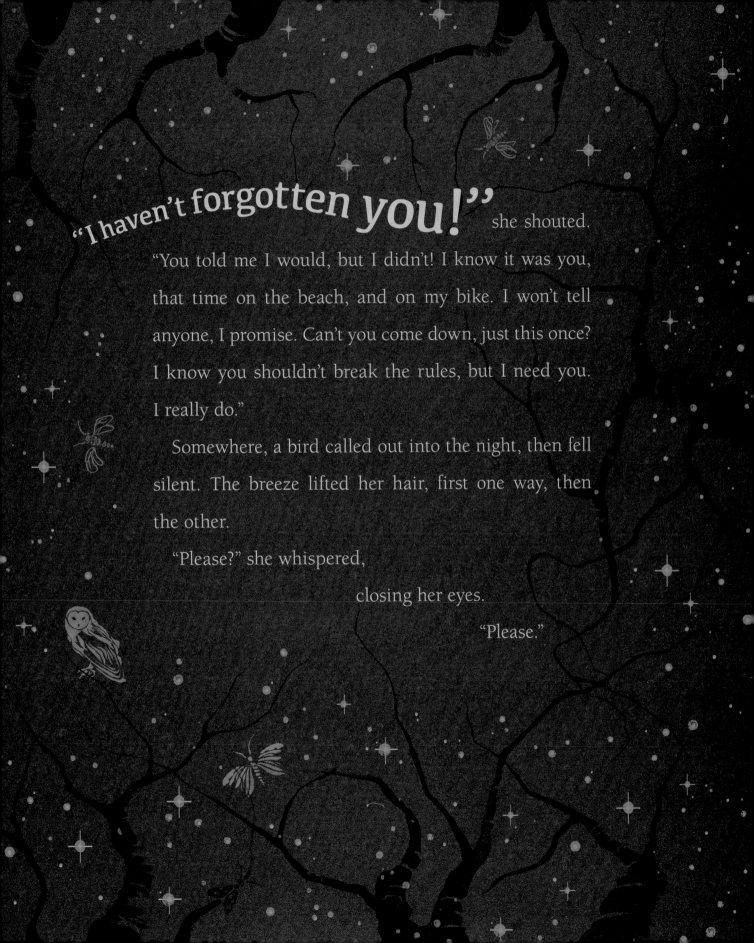

"I haven't forgotten **you!**" she shouted.
"You told me I would, but I didn't! I know it was you,
that time on the beach, and on my bike. I won't tell
anyone, I promise. Can't you come down, just this once?
I know you shouldn't break the rules, but I need you.
I really do."

Somewhere, a bird called out into the night, then fell
silent. The breeze lifted her hair, first one way, then
the other.

"Please?" she whispered,

closing her eyes.

"Please."

There was a blast of chill air, a clatter, and a great clap, like thunder, and there he was, crouching on the icy grass, his robes pooled around him, his wing feathers fluttering in the air.

"Here I am," he said, straightening up, brushing down his robes, darting quick looks around the garden. "Now, I'm going to have to ask you to keep the noise down. You really do have a very clear speaking voice. Hasn't anyone ever told y—?"

"Snow Angel!" she cried, and she ran towards him, throwing her arms around him, even though he was freezing and not the sort of person who liked hugs.

The snow angel gave a yelp of surprise. Then, after a moment, he patted her with his cold, cold hands.

"There, there," he said. "All's well. I told you I'd come if you needed me, didn't I?"

She wouldn't let go, telling him how grateful she was to him for saving her from the wave, for pushing her bicycle off the path.

"Don't mention it. Really. Just doing my job," he said, easing her arms off him. "Nice of you to say it and all that, but there's no need to fuss. You must let me go. You might melt me."

Instantly, Sylvie withdrew and stood apart from him, looking up at his pale, chiseled face.

He gazed back at her, a frown puckering his brow. "What is all this? How come you are out here, on your own, in the dark? It's freezing and you should be in bed, not gallivanting about in the middle of the night." The snow angel placed a hand on her brow and peered into her eyes like a doctor. "What's wrong? Are you in some sort of danger that I can't see? Do you have a pain anywhere?"

"No, I'm fine," Sylvie said.

"Fine?" he asked, raising one icy eyebrow. "Do you mean 'fine' like the time you were ill? Or 'fine' like you were at the top of that tree?"

"I really am all right this time," she said. "I promise you. I'm just . . . worried. There's something I can't stop thinking about and I need to ask you a favor. A sort of wish."

"A wish?" he repeated in an offended tone. "Do I look like a genie from a bottle? You can't summon me for a wish. That's not how this works. You're going to get me into trouble again. A snow angel is more of a—"

"I'm sorry," Sylvie cried. "I didn't mean to get you into trouble. I really wanted to see you again and—"

"Shhh," the angel said with a hasty glance at the sky. "You need to lower your voice. We're not supposed to talk to each other. You know that."

"Sorry," she whispered. "It's quite a big favor. I don't know if you can do it, but there's nobody else I can ask."

The snow angel sighed. He walked over to the low wall of the rockery and sat down.

"You know," he said, "other snow angels visit their makers only once in a while. They drift down, do a short task, save them from harm, and back they go. Swift, to the point, no one any the wiser. But you? From the very start, you were different." He gazed at her narrowly. "I really don't know why. Not only do you see me and speak to me and remember me, but you seem to get yourself into more scrapes than seem possible. Why did I have to be made by someone who would keep me so busy?"

Sylvie went over to him. "I'm sorry," she said again, taking his hand. "I don't mean to get into scrapes. I just miss you when you're not here."

"But I'm always here," he said.

Sylvie shifted her weight from one foot to the other. She thought that if she could just keep hold of his cold, snowy palm, like this, he might remain here with her forever.

"I have to go soon," the angel said, as if he had read her thoughts.

"Do you?"

"You know I do." He peered quickly up at the sky, before leaning forwards a little. "Shall I tell you something?" he said in a whisper.

"What?" she whispered back. "Is it a secret?"

"Yes." He stole another glance upwards. "Sometimes . . ."
He hesitated. "Sometimes . . . I'm glad you didn't forget me."

Sylvie clutched his icy fingers very tightly and closed her eyes. "Me too," she managed to say.

They remained like that for a moment, the angel sitting on the rockery wall, with Sylvie before him, the garden around them glinting with frost.

"Time to go," he said eventually. "You'd better tell me your wish."

"Really?" Sylvie's eyes sprang open. "You mean it?"

"I can't promise anything, but tell me anyway."

"Sure?"

"Yes. Go on. You might as well, now I'm here."

Sylvie rested her hand lightly on his shoulder and whispered her wish into his ear.

When she had finished, the snow angel turned his head towards her. His face was doubtful, his brow furrowed.

"I don't know about that," he said. "It's never been done before. No one else has ever asked for that."

Sylvie folded her hands together. "I know you can do it."

"We'll see," he said. "I'll have to ask around."

The next morning, Sylvie knew before she pulled back the curtains; she recognized that silence, that stillness, that blue-tinged light. It was as if a blanket had fallen over the world.

She leaped out of bed and yanked back her curtains. The pavements were gone, the cars turned into sleeping, hunched white dragons, trees bent low with the weight of snow.

"You did it!" she shouted. "You did it!" Then she ran into her parents' room, dragging the covers off their bed, saying they had to get up, they had to get up now, and come outside.

She put on her thickest socks, her wooliest mittens, her warmest coat, and her coziest hat and ran out into the snow.

Sylvie had to find everyone she knew. She had to tell them to get out into the snow, to lie back, to move their arms and legs, to make themselves a snow angel.

Quick, she would tell them, before the snow melts. It was going to be a busy day.

Later that night, when Sylvie and her parents and everyone else in the town was asleep, the snow from the snow angel's blizzard began to thaw and melt. It slid off the trees, it dripped from gutters, it turned to slush on the roads. It vanished in patches from pavements and gardens, the lawns reappearing, the stones uncovering themselves. Snowflake by snowflake, the thick white snow disappeared, back to where it had come from.

Last to melt were the angels in the snow. Slowly, slowly, ever so slowly, they faded and dissolved: first their wings, then their faces, then their robes. They vanished into the air, merged with the breezes, mingled with the wind, rising up, and up, and up, to re-form in the sky, right above their makers.

Have you ever woken
suddenly, in the middle of the
night, without knowing why?
It's only your snow angel
passing through, paying
you a visit.

AUTHOR'S NOTE

Where Snow Angels Go began life as a bedtime story I made up
for my own children. The character of the Snow Angel first came
to me when I was in the back of an ambulance with my daughter,
on the way to hospital. She was in anaphylactic shock, feeling very
frightened and very cold. On the spur of the moment, to distract
and divert her, I said, "You're going to be fine—it's just a snow
angel wrapping his wings around you." Instantly, her face cleared,
and you could just see her thinking about this angel instead of
what was happening to her. "Tell me more," she said. And so I did.
The story grew and grew, and eventually my children wanted to
see pictures to go with the words. Daniela stepped in to help me
here, luckily—I cannot draw to save my life!